ARDIANE AND BARBE BLEUE

OR,

THE USELESS DELIVERANCE

Ardiane and Barbe Bleue

❧ ❧ *Translated into English*
Verse from the Manuscript
of Maurice Maeterlinck ❧ ❧

❧ ❧ *By* Bernard Miall ❧ ❧

Fredonia Books
Amsterdam, The Netherlands

Ardiane & Barbe Bleue

by
Maurice Maeterlinck

ISBN 1-58963-395-4

Translated into English Verse from the Manuscripts
by Bernard Miall

Reprinted from the Original edition

Fredonia Books
Amsterdam, The Netherlands
http://www.fredoniabooks.com

TRANSLATOR'S PREFACE

I

"THESE two little plays," * says the author, "are really librettos. Music is being written to them by M. Gilkas." The French version is in unrhymed alexandrines, if the term be permissible; that is, in unrhymed lines of twelve syllables. It is of course possible to employ this metre in English verse, but it is a medium as yet too little polished by use to refract, without theft or distortion, its immanent sense; it is, so to speak, one of your material metres, more ready to present itself in body than in spirit, being still in a primitive stage of evolution, and waiting the master-hand which shall teach it an easy delivery and self-effacement. In short, it is a metre neither so far familiar nor so far developed as to justify its use by a translator, whose duty is to interpret his author, in some remote degree, as his author might wish, rather than to experiment as himself might please.

For myself, I had no envy to attempt it, and so, with my author's approval, I have turned his play into such blank verse as I might; holding, with him, that our English unrhymed verse of ten syllables, iambic in scheme,—trochaic, dactylic, anapæstic, catalectic, and what not by incident,—is an equivalent sufficiently near, and perhaps the most proper, of the French unrhymed verse of twelve syllables. But I do not pretend that the author's mood may not be betrayed by the staccato effect of the shorter line. To the French alexandrine, of all metres, is possible at times a "linkéd sweetness long drawn out," which by a shorter metre, or, indeed, by any metre consisting, as ours, very largely of accent, is rarely attainable.

Readers may miss in "Sister Beatrice" what they are used to call the glamour, the atmosphere, of the Maeterlinckian drama. They will miss it partly, no doubt, because I have translated it; but partly also because it is partly absent in the French; they may, perhaps, find more of it in the music, if they have the fortune to hear it. But the play unsung, unstaged,—it is, as I have said, a libretto—is the play of M. Maeterlinck's which most nearly approaches, in the matter of treatment, the avowedly obvious spirit of the English drama. That the story is all spiritual, or rather, that the spiritual in the play has a story, is no doubt the reason why the treatment may be material and articulate.

Translator's Preface

Other plays of this author might be described — he himself, I think, might so describe them—as belonging to static or potential drama : the plays were the dramas of a state of feeling. Here, I think, we have for the first time in M. Maeterlinck's theatre the treatment of a legend already crystallised : a legend in England familiar to readers of Mr. John Davidson's poetry in "The Ballad of a Nun." It has also been treated by Miss Adelaide Anne Procter, and a singularly charming translation of the original Dutch version — for in Dutch we find it first told and first printed— may be found in the first volume of a publication called the "Pageant," issued some years ago. This version was translated by Mr. Laurence Housman and Mr. J. Simons ; whether it be the oldest or the original version I am unable to say.

Translator's Preface

This to explain why "Sister Beatrice" is not most obviously by M. Maeterlinck, and by no one else.

LIDO, VENICE,
     May 10, 1900.

II

IN translating "Ardiane and Barbe Bleue," which, like "Sister Beatrice," was written as a libretto, I have again used the ordinary "blank verse" line to represent the unrhymed French line of twelve syllables. But in the original text of this drama there are many passages in *vers libre*, both rhymed and otherwise. To make irregular metres readable in English requires no less than inspiration, and if inspiration is not always at the service of the poet it is still less often at the beck of the translator. In such passages I have therefore preserved, so far as possible, the original measures, but have in all cases, or nearly all, retained or added rhyme.

It was not easy to decide whether I should call our familiar hero-villain Blue-beard or Barbe Bleue. As children we connect him with Ali Baba and the Forty Thieves; but if he be anything less than universal he would appear to be French. Some would relegate him merely to the post of an accidentally baptized variety of the Myth of the Closed Chamber;[1] some identify him with a certain Marshal and Constable of France,[2] companion-in-arms to the Duke of Brittany; some say he is Henry VIII.; at all events one

[1] See "The Forbidden Chamber": E. Sidney Hartland, *Folk-lore Journal*, 1885, vol. iii. Also Mr. Lang's edition of Perrault. It was from Perrault that M. Maeterlinck obtained the legend, which he has altered to suit himself.

[2] See "Un Maréchal et un Connétable de France. La Barbe Bleue de la légende et de l'histoire," in the British Museum.

Translator's Preface

Gilles de Lavalle, sieur de Rais, and lord in all of some eight goodly châteaux, for the most part in Brittany, constable and marshal as aforesaid, did commit certain atrocities upon certain women and children, though his wife survived him, and he was in 1440 executed therefor, at the age of thirty-six. One popular legend has it that the brothers of seven deceased wives arrived with Saint Gildas, whereupon the castle crumbled away, and the brothers killed the marshal and constable. Whether this feudal dignitary, who in his twenties was marshal, constable, and councillor to King Charles VII., was or was not the original of the Bluebeard legend, it is certain that of the ruins of his numerous castles all are known by the latter's name, and are connected with legends of his atrocities; and in one, the castle of Chantocé, which one Thiphaine or Triphine d'Anguille gave in 1100 to

the forebears of one Marie de Crain, who
in marriage brought it to Gui, father of
Rais, father of Barbe Bleue, or Gilles
de Lavalle, may be seen to this day a
long subterranean hall, communicating
with another, low and square, which is
entered by three staircases. Chantocé is
built on a flat rock, surrounded by a moat,
and was defended by two towers with
drawbridges. It is interesting to note
that the depravity of Gilles was attributed
to the fervent study of pernicious litera-
ture in his youth.

As the story of Bluebeard pure and
simple, as distinguished from that of
Bluebeard Gilles, is found in Greek,
French, Tuscan, Icelandic, Esthonian,
Gaelic, and Basque, it seems unlikely that
Gilles was the origin of the legend. It
is most likely that the Myth of the Forbidden Chamber found, as all stories will
sooner or later find, an exposition in

actual life; so that the real drama, in course of years and popular relation, took to itself some or all of the international Forbidden Chamber details, while the Forbidden Chamber stories were given, in many countries, a name, and in France a local habitation—or rather some eight or nine such.

The name of the victorious and final wife is variable. Often it is Anne. Sometimes she finds the corpses, sometimes the heads; the wives, who are usually seven, are sometimes her sisters and sometimes not. Sometimes her brothers kill the polygamous husband; sometimes she has no brothers, and restores the wives to life, as she does in one of the Gaelic versions. In the version of Perrault, which is probably the original of all our English versions, she finds the bodies of the wives, and her brothers execute justice.

Translator's Preface

When I thought of retaining the French name of the hero, it was, as I say, to preserve the reader from reminiscences of the pantomime and the Arabian Nights, which somehow do not "march together" with the drama of M. Maeterlinck. I finally determined to retain "Barbe Bleue" for the name of our hero because the names of all the other characters are French, and untranslatable, and it seemed to me that the contrast of the English name of our hero would still further accentuate the illegitimate Arabian and pantomimic reminiscences that, for some of us, cling to it. Plain "Bluebeard" is hardly congruous with these other names; we have never thought of our childhood's monster as the warden of a harem of maidens out of a play by M. Maeterlinck. The point is difficult as it is nice, and also trivial, and perhaps it is best to leave the reader to give our hero the name that

his individual taste dictates. My apology
is to disarm the captious.

A word as to the versification of these
two translations. They are for the most
part written in what is popularly called
" blank verse." At the same time, be-
sides employing the slight variations
which precedence allows in such verse, I
have introduced, here and there, what I
conceive to be a variation especially desir-
able in a translation, wherein one cannot
always, or often, choose one's words, and
is sometimes compelled to employ a phrase
that would, if handled in the ordinary
way, be unmusical in the extreme. This
variation consists in the employment of
the well-known principle of catalexis where
not to employ that principle would result
in cacophony. To render certain conca-
tenations of consonants, especially those
containing sibilants, tolerable to the ear, I
have allowed for the time which their

pronunciation actually demands, by counting them as a syllable, so that the deca-syllabic line, though still having the time of ten syllables, has only nine syllables in it if estimated in the ordinary way. An example of such a line is :—

"In silence shed before a queen's feet."

Another example is—

"Open the fifth door."—"Not even there ?"

I should not have referred to this matter had not a critic quoted one of the above lines as a proof that I was ignorant of the elementary rules of versification.

BERNARD MIALL.

LONDON, *April* 18, 1901.

* The Preface refers to two plays, as it originally appeared in an edition combining:

Sister Beatrice and *Ardiane & Barbe Bleue*

ARDIANE AND BARBE BLEUE

OR,

THE USELESS DELIVERANCE

THE PERSONS OF THE PLAY

ARDIANE
SELYSETTE
MELISANDE
YGRAINE
BELLANGERE
ALLADINE
A NURSE (foster-mother to ARDIANE)

BARBE BLEUE

Peasants, the Crowd.

ARDIANE AND BARBE BLEUE

ACT THE FIRST

A vast, resplendent hall, of semi-circular form, in the castle of Barbe Bleue. *At the remoter end, in the centre of the semi-circular wall, is an enormous door ; on either hand of this are three smaller doors, of ebony, with locks and ornaments of silver ; each door is set within a niche, and all these niches are enclosed by a semi-circular colonnade of marble, the pillars of which support the balcony overhead. Above these doors, but set further back, are six great windows, to which the aforesaid balcony gives access ; these may be gained*

3

from either side of the hall, by two
flights of stairs, which follow the curve
of the walls, and lead up to the semi-
circular gallery.

It is evening ; the great windows are open,
and the candelabra lit. Without,
below the windows, is an invisible,
excited crowd, whose cries, now uneasy,
now terrified, now threatening, together
with the sound of sudden movements,
the trampling of feet, and the murmur
of persons speaking, are heard with
great distinctness. During the first
bars of the overture the curtain rises,
and the voices of the hidden crowd are
at once heard above the music.

VOICES IN THE CROWD

So . . . she was in the chariot ? Did
you see ?
All the village lingered there,
There, to see her. . . Is she fair ?

She looked at me. . . . And me. . . . And me.
O miserable child ! . . . Yet all the while
She seemed to smile.
Whence hath she come ? . . . From very
    far away,
To know not . . . what awaits her here
    to-day.
Their journey hath endured for thrice
    ten days. . . .
He cannot see us . . . shout, that he may
    know. . . .

                           [*All together.*

Back ! Back ! . . . Advance no nearer !
    Never go
Up to the castle ! . . . It is death, death,
    death !

                          [*Isolated voices.*

She does not understand. . . . I hear they
    say
No less than twenty men pursued her way,
That dwelt about her home. . . . You
    wonder why ?

Because they loved her. . . . Many used to
    cry
Along the roads. . . . Why has she come,
    O why ?
They tell me that she knew. . . . He shall
    not have her, no !
She is too fair for you ! . . . He shall
    not have her, no ! . . .
O see them, see them, there they go !
Where are they going ? . . . They are
    coming through,
By the red gate. . . . It is not true . . .
I see their torches in the avenue !
There the great chariot goes between the
    trees !
He is afraid. . . . He shall not have her, no !
He is mad, mad, mad ! He is mad ! He
    has done enough !
It is too much ! . . . So she will be the
    sixth !
O murderer, butcher ! . . . Death to the
    butcher, death !

6

Ardiane and Barbe Bleue

Fire, fire! . . . Bring fire! . . . I have
    brought my hay-fork, see!
And I my scythe!—They are entering
    the yard . . .
Hey, let me see! . . . Take care! . . .
    The gates are barred!
Wait for them here. . . . They say she
    knows it all!
What does she know? . . . She knows
    what I know too. . . .
What do you know? . . . I know they
    all are dead!
Not dead, not dead? . . . I buried them
    myself!
But I one evening once as I went by
Heard singing voices. . . . So did I. . . .
    And I . . .
Ay, they come back, they say. . . . But he
Brings down misfortune on our heads. . . .
    O see,
The windows! . . . They are closing of
    themselves!

Ardiane and Barbe Bleue

Now . . . they are going in! They are
    going in. . . .
Nothing to see! . . . Death to him!
    Death! Death! Death!
> [*And at this moment the six great
> windows above the interior bal-
> cony close of their own motion,
> stifling little by little the voices
> of the crowd. Soon nothing is
> heard but an indefinite murmur
> which is almost silence. Shortly
> afterwards* ARDIANE *and the*
> NURSE *enter by a side door.*

THE NURSE

Where are we? . . . Listen! . . . Ah! . . .
    that muttering there!
It is the peasants : they were eager, yes,
To save us : yes, they ran along the roads,
But never dared to speak : they made us
    signs,

8

They made us signs that meant we should
    return. . . .
        [*She goes forward to the great door
            at the end of the hall.*
They are here, behind this door ! . . . I
    hear them : some
Tramp to and fro. . . . Now let us try
    to flee. . . .
He leaves us here alone : we can escape,
Perhaps. . . . I tell you plainly, he is
    mad !
O, it is death ! For all they say is true,
He has killed five women. . .

Ardiane

                No, they are not dead . . .
Yonder I heard it spoken of at times,
In the far place whereto his savage love,
That yet was tremulous, came to seek me
    out,
As of a thing incomprehensible.
I was suspicious of the truth, and here

9

Am sure. He loves me : I am beautiful :
So shall I learn his secret. But ere all
We must be insubordinate. When the
    future
Is threatening to us and inscrutable
That is ere all our duty. For the rest,
They were mistaken; and if they are
    lost
They were lost by hesitation.

                              Here are we,
Within the outer hall whence opens out
The chamber where his love awaits me.
    Here
Are keys he gave me of the treasure-
    chests
Of bridal raiment, and the silver keys
Are ours to use : the golden is forbid.
That is the only one of import. These,
The six, I cast away : the last I keep.

              [*She throws away the keys of silver,*
                   which tinkle and ring on the
                   marble flags.

10

Ardiane and Barbe Bleue

THE NURSE (*who hastily picks them up again*)

What are you doing? He has given you
The treasures, all the treasures that they
open!

ARDIANE

Open them you, then, if it give you
pleasure;
For me, I seek for the forbidden door.
Open the others if you will; but all
That is permitted us will tell us nought.

THE NURSE (*looking at the keys and then about the hall*)

The doors are yonder, set within the
marble,
And we may know, since all have locks of
silver,
They answer to the keys: but first of all,
Which one shall I unclose?

Ardiane and Barbe Bleue

ARDIANE

What matter which?
They are but there to turn aside our
    minds
From that we need to know. . . . I do
    not find,
Although I seek for it, the seventh
    door. . . .

THE NURSE (*trying the lock of the
    first door*)

Is this the key of the first? . . . Or this?
    . . . Or this?
Not yet, not yet. . . . Ay, but the third
    goes in,
Dragging my fingers after it! . . . Be-
    ware! . . .
Fly! . . . The two panels both have
    come to life!
They are gliding back like curtains! . . .
    What is this?

12

Ardiane and Barbe Bleue

Beware, beware! . . . It is a hail of fire,
That beats upon my hands, that wounds
    my face!
O!

    [*The* NURSE *springs backward, for
while she is speaking the two
leaves of the door glide of their
own motion into lateral re-
cesses, and suddenly disappear,
disclosing a vast heap of
amethysts piled up to the top
of the doorway. Then, as
though delivered suddenly from
centuries of constraint, count-
less gems and jewels of every
size and form, but all of the
one substance, amethyst—neck-
laces, bracelets, rings, aigrettes,
buckles, girdles, collars, diadems
—fall like a crumbling mass of
violet flames, and rebound as
far as the further side of the*

13

*hall ; and, while the first to
fall spread themselves over the
marble flags, others, more and
more numerous and more and
more resplendent, begin to fall
from all the mouldings of the
enchanted vaultings, and flow
therefrom continually with an
incessant sound of living jewels.*

THE NURSE (*fascinated, bewildered, gather-
ing up jewels with both her hands*)

Gather them up, O stoop, gather them
    up !
Take the most beautiful ! Enough are
    here
To glorify a kingdom !   Still they fall !
They pierce my hair, they stone my hands !
    O look !
Unheard-of gems are raining from the
    vaults,

14

Ardiane and Barbe Bleue

Miraculous violets, purple, lilac, mauve !
Plunge your arms into them and hide your
    face,
And I will fill my mantle full with them !

ARDIANE

These amethysts are noble.   Open now
The second door.

THE NURSE

      The second ?   I dare not ! . . .
Yet I would know if . . .
     [*She inserts the key in the lock of the*
       second door.
              O, beware, beware !
The key already turns !   And they have
    wings,
The doors : the walls too tear themselves
    asunder !
O !
     [*The scene is the same as on the*
       opening of the first door, but

this time is seen the accumu-
lated wealth, the rebounding
irruption, the dazzling and
musical fall of a blue rain of
sapphires.

ARDIANE

These are fine sapphires. Open now the
    third.

THE NURSE

Wait, wait until I see that I have here
Indeed the most magnificent. My cloak
Will break beneath the weight of blue,
    blue sky!
O see them overflow! on every hand
They pour, pour, pour!—a violet torrent
    here,
And yonder in a stream of azure blue!

ARDIANE

Come, come, Nurse, quickly, for the
    chance to sin
Is rare and fugitive. . . .

16

Ardiane and Barbe Bleue

THE NURSE (*opens the third door, when
the same thing befalls, save that
this time follows the pale invasion,
the milky rush, of a deluge of pearls,
a shower less heavy, but more illimit-
able than those preceding*)

                    I will but take
A handful of them, so they may caress
The sapphires.

ARDIANE

Open now the fourth door.

THE NURSE (*opens the fourth door, when
as before there is a shower of jewels,
but this time of emeralds*)

O, these are greener than the Spring that
    runs
Along the poplars thick with drops of
    dew

Ardiane and Barbe Bleue

That catch the lovely sunlight in my
    home !
      [*Shaking her mantle, which over-*
         flows with amethysts, sapphires,
         and pearls.
Away, away, ye others ! give you place
For the most beautiful — for I was
    born
Under the boughs, and love the light of
    leaves.

ARDIANE

Open the fifth door.

THE NURSE

           O, not even these ?
You do not love them ?

ARDIANE

        What I love is fair
Beyond all fairness of miraculous gems.

18

Ardiane and Barbe Bleue

THE NURSE (*opening the fifth door, to set free a blinding irruption, a living incandescence, a sinister deluge and cascade of rubies*)

O, these are terrible : I will not touch !

ARDIANE

Now we approach the end : the threat lies here.
Open the sixth.

THE NURSE

It is the last key.

ARDIANE

Open it quickly.
[*The* NURSE, *hesitating, opens the sixth door. All passes as before : but the radiance is this time intolerable. Cataracts of enormous diamonds of the first*

19

water pour into the hall; myriads
of sparks, flashes, flecks of fire,
and prismatic rays mingle, are
extinguished, blaze forth again
and multiply, outspreading as
they fall. ARDIANE, *startled,*
gives a dazed cry. She stoops,
picks up a diadem, a necklace,
and handfuls of the glistening
splendour, and therewith she
decks at random her hair, her
arms, her throat, her hands.
Then, flashing before her eyes
and raising before her face
diamonds that shed a brilliance
upon her.

O, my flashing diamonds!
For you I never sought, but on my way
I greet you! O immortal dew of light!
Stream o'er my hands, illuminate my arms,
Dazzle my very flesh! O, you are pure,
And you are tireless, and you never die:

Ardiane and Barbe Bleue

And that which in your fires eternally
Trembles, like to a populace of spirits,
That have constrained and wear the stars
    of Heaven,
It is the passion of that Radiance
Which, penetrating all things, knows no
    rest,
And finds no more to conquer, save itself!
      [She approaches the door, and looks
          up at the vaulted arch.

Rain on, O supreme heart of summer,
    rain!
O shards of light, O limitless soul of flame!
Yea, wound my eyes, yet shall you never
    tire
Those eyes of gazing!
            [Leaning yet further back.
               O, what is it there?
O Nurse, where are you? For the
    splendid rain
Hangs motionless, suspended in a bow,
A diamond rainbow of prismatic fire! . . .

Ardiane and Barbe Bleue

O see the seventh door, with golden bars,
With golden lock and hinges!

The Nurse

                      Come away!
No, never touch it!   No, withdraw your
    hands!
Withdraw your eyes, lest of itself it open!
Come, let us hide!   These diamonds—
    after them
Or fire will come, or death!

Ardiane

                 Go back, go back!
Hide you yourself behind a marble shaft:
I will alone go forward.

        [*She steps into the recess under the
            vaulted doorway, and inserts
            the key in the lock. The door
            divides into two panels, and
            disappears: nothing is visible*

save an opening full of dark-
ness : but the sound of singing,
muffled and remote, rises from
the depths of the earth, and
spreads through the hall.

THE NURSE

Ardiane !
What are you doing ? Is it you that
sings ?

ARDIANE

Listen !

THE DISTANT VOICES

Orlamonde's five daughters,
When the faery died,
Orlamonde's five daughters
Sought to win outside.

THE NURSE

They are . . . the other women !

ARDIANE

Yes.

23

Ardiane and Barbe Bleue

THE NURSE

O, shut the door! Their singing fills
 the hall:
It will be heard, heard everywhere!

ARDIANE (*trying to close the door*)

I cannot!

THE DISTANT VOICES

They lit their five lanterns,
   Through all the towers they sought,
And in four hundred chambers;
   The day, they found it not.

THE NURSE

Now it is louder, always louder! Come!
Come, let us close—help me—the outer
 door. . . .
   [*They try to close the door that con-
   cealed the diamonds.*

This too resists!   We cannot shut them
   in !

The Distant Voices

Then they found an echoing deep,
   And let it them enfold :
And upon a stubborn door
   Found a key of gold.

The Nurse (*bewildered, and also entering the recess*)

Be silent, silent ! . . . We shall all be
   lost !
Stifle that voice !

         [*Stretching out her mantle.*
       The doorway—ah, my cloak
Will cover it. . . .

Ardiane

      I see beyond the sill
Steps. I am going down to where they
   sing.

Ardiane and Barbe Bleue

THE DISTANT VOICES (*always louder*).
Through the chinks they see the ocean :
    Ah, they fear to die !
They strike the door they dare not open,
    And the hours go by.
> [*At the last words of the song* BARBE
> BLEUE *enters the hall. For a
> moment he stops short, gazing ;
> then he draws near to the women.*

BARBE BLEUE.

You too !

ARDIANE (*who starts, leaves the doorway,
and advances, glittering with diamonds,
towards* BARBE BLEUE)

    I above all.

BARBE BLEUE

            I thought that you
Were stronger, wiser than your sisters were.

Ardiane and Barbe Bleue

ARDIANE

How long did they avoid the thing forbid ?

BARBE BLEUE

This, for some days ; that, a few months ;
    and one,
The last of all, a year.

ARDIANE

          It was the last,
Only the last, that there was need to punish.

BARBE BLEUE

It was a very little thing to ask.

ARDIANE

You asked of these more than you ever
    gave.

BARBE BLEUE

The happiness I willed for you you lose.

27

Ardiane and Barbe Bleue

ARDIANE

The happiness I would lives not in dark
ness.

When I know all to pardon will be
mine.

BARBE BLEUE (*seizing* ARDIANE *by the arm*)

Come! Come!

ARDIANE

Where would you, then, that I should go?

BARBE BLEUE

Where I shall lead you.

ARDIANE

No.

> [BARBE BLEUE *strives to drag her
> away by force. She gives a
> long cry of pain. This cry is
> answered at first by a low*

murmur from without. The struggle between the two continues for a few moments, and the Nurse *gives vent to despairing outcries. Suddenly a stone, hurled from without, shatters one of the windows, and the crowd is heard, excited and enraged. Other stones fall; the* Nurse, *running to the great door at the end of the hall, raises the bars and shoots the bolts. A sudden rush from outside splinters the door and forces it in; and the peasants, infuriated but hesitating, crowd upon the threshold.* Barbe Bleue, *releasing* Ardiane, *draws his sword and prepares for the onset. But* Ardiane, *tranquil, advances towards the crowd.*

29

Ardiane and Barbe Bleue

ARDIANE

What would you?   He has not done me
any ill.

> [*She gently disperses the peasants,
> and carefully closes the door,
> while* BARBE BLEUE, *with
> lowered eyes, gazes at the point
> of his sword.*

CURTAIN

ACT THE SECOND

*At the rising of the curtain the scene is a
vast subterranean hall, with a vaulted
roof supported by many columns ; it
is plunged in almost total darkness.
From the extreme right, almost in the
wings, there runs back a narrow, wind-
ing subterranean passage, also with a
vaulted roof ; it debouches into the
great hall towards the front of the
stage by a roughly-arched opening.*

At the further end of this passage ARDIANE
and the NURSE *are seen, descending the
last few steps of a stairway ;* ARDIANE
carries a lamp.

THE NURSE

Hush !   Do you hear ?   He shuts the
iron door

31

Over our heads! Why would you not
    give way?
We never shall behold the day again.

ARDIANE

Fear not; he is wounded, he is overcome;
But knows it not as yet. With supplication
He will re-open it : but let us seek
First if we cannot of ourselves win free.
Meanwhile his wrath all that his love
    refused
Has granted : we shall find what here is hid.
      [*She advances, holding the lamp high
         above her head, to the mouth
         of the passage, and there bends
         forward, seeking to penetrate
         the darkness of the hall. At
         the first ray of light which
         pierces the obscurity is heard
         the sound of hushed and fearful
         flight. ARDIANE turns towards
         the NURSE to call her.*

Ardiane and Barbe Bleue

ARDIANE

Come! They are here!
> [*She enters the hall which the lamp illuminates pillar by pillar.*

Where are you?
> [*A terrified moan replies.* ARDIANE *directs the rays of her lamp toward the part from which it seems to proceed, and perceives the forms of five women, motionless with fright, who are huddled together in the shadows of the remotest pillars.*

ARDIANE (*in a muffled voice, still half fearful*)

They are there!
Nurse, nurse, where are you?
> [*The* NURSE *hastens toward* ARDIANE: ARDIANE *gives her*

33

*the lamp, and takes a few
hesitating steps toward the five.*

Sisters, O my sisters !

[*The five start.*

They live ! They live ! They live ! Behold
me here !

[*She runs to them with open arms,
clasps them with hesitating
hands, strains them to her
breast, and kisses them and
caresses them, feeling about her
with uncertain gestures, in a
kind of impassioned and con-
vulsive tenderness, while the
NURSE, lamp in hand, stands
still a little apart.*

ARDIANE

O, I have you ! . . . They are full of life,
They are full of sweetness ! . . . When
    I saw the hall
Open in darkness from the passage end,

Ardiane and Barbe Bleue

I thought to find . . . ah me ! . . . dead
    bodies here. . . .
And lo . . . I kiss these loveliest lips in
    tears !
Have you not suffered ? O, your lips
    how fresh,
Your cheeks how like the cheeks of
    children ! See,
Your naked arms are supple, ay, and
    warm ;
Your round round breasts are throbbing
    through their veils !
Why do you tremble ? . . . O, how
    many you are !
Now I clasp shoulders ; now my arms
    entwine
Hips, and my touch on whom I know
    not rests. . . .
On every hand my lips meet lips, my
    breast meets breasts.
O this that bathes you all, this hair !
You must be fair, so fair !

Ardiane and Barbe Bleue

Waves, faintly warm, are parted by my
    hands,
My arms are lost amid rebellious strands. . . .
Have you a thousand tresses? . . . and
    are they
Like night, or like the day?
I see no longer what I do,
But I am kissing, kissing all of you,
And one by one I gather all your hands!
It is the least of you I find the last:
O never tremble! See, I hold you fast,
My arms enfold you close to me!
Nurse, nurse, what are you doing there?
Behold me like a mother here,
Feeling in darkness, and my children . . .
    they
Await the dawn to clear.

       [*The* NURSE *draws near, bearing the
           lamp, and its light falls on the
           group of women. The captives
           are then seen to be clad in rags,
           their hair in disorder, their*

> *faces emaciated and their eyes*
> *dazzled and alarmed.* ARDI-
> ANE, *for a moment astonished,*
> *takes the lamp from the* NURSE,
> *in order the better to light them,*
> *and to regard them more*
> *closely.*

ARDIANE

O, you have suffered here!
And O, how gloomy does your prison
    seem!
Great clammy drops are falling on my
    hands,
And my lamp's flame is flickering all the
    while!
How strange your eyes are when you look
    at me!
And you draw back as I approach—but
    why?
What, are you still afraid?
And who is that who seeks to fly?

I

Ardiane and Barbe Bleue

Is it not she, the youngest of you all,
She that I kissed but now?
O, has my long long sister's kiss
Done to you any harm?
Come to me, come then! Do you fear
    the light?
Tell me, what is her name?

Two or Three Timid Voices

Selysette.

ARDIANE

Selysette—a smile?
It is the first that I have seen this while!
Your wide eyes falter as though they saw
    the Dead,
Although in truth they look on life in-
    stead:
And O, these delicate bare arms that
    tremble,
Both waiting to be loved! Come, my arms
    too

Are waiting, though I tremble not as you !
                    [*Embracing her.*
You have been in this tomb how many
    days ?

SELYSETTE

We count the days but ill here, oftentimes
Deceive ourselves, but none the less I think
I have been here for upwards of a year.

    [YGRAINE *advances : she is paler than
    the others.*

ARDIANE

It is a long while since you saw the light !

YGRAINE

I used not to unclose my eyes ; I wept
So long alone.

SELYSETTE (*looking fixedly at* ARDIANE)
                    How beautiful you are !
How could he bring himself to punish you
As he used us ?   You also in the end
Have disobeyed him ?

39

Ardiane and Barbe Bleue

ARDIANE

                    No, it was not so !
No, I obeyed more swiftly than the rest,
But other laws than his.

SELYSETTE

                    Why have you come ?
O why have you come here ?

ARDIANE

                    To set you free.

SELYSETTE

How should we be set free ?

ARDIANE

                    But follow me :
No more than that. . . . What used you
     here to do ?

SELYSETTE

We prayed, sang, wept, and then we waited
     always.

Ardiane and Barbe Bleue

ARDIANE

You never sought escape?

SELYSETTE

We could not flee,
For all the ways are shut, and flight forbid.

ARDIANE

That we shall see. . . . But she that looks
    at me
Between the tangles of her fallen hair
That seems to wrap her round in frozen
    flame—
What is her name?

SELYSETTE

Her name is Melisande.

ARDIANE

Come hither, Melisande!   And she whose
    eyes,
Wide, eager eyes, are following my lamp?

41

Ardiane and Barbe Bleue

SELYSETTE

Bellangere.

ARDIANE

      And that other, who is hid
Behind the heavy pillar?

SELYSETTE

              She has come
From very far away, poor Alladine!

ARDIANE

Why do you call her poor?

SELYSETTE

            Because she came
Last of us all, and speaks another tongue.

ARDIANE (*holding out her arms to*
ALLADINE)

Come, Alladine! . . . You see that I speak
    hers,
When I embrace her thus.

42

Ardiane and Barbe Bleue

SELYSETTE

                She has not yet
Ever ceased weeping.

ARDIANE (*looking at* SELYSETTE *and the
      others with astonishment*)

              Why, but you yourself,
Can you not laugh yet—laugh and clap
    your hands?
And all the rest are silent!   What is this?
What are you?   Will you live in terror
    thus
Always?   I do not see you smile at all,
While with your eyes—incredulous eyes!
    —you watch
My every gesture.   Will you not believe
The joyful news?   O, do you not regret
The light of day, the birds among the
    boughs,
The high green gardens blowing over-
    head?

43

Ardiane and Barbe Bleue

Do you not know the world is in the
    Spring?
I yester-morning, wandering by the way,
Drank in the light, the sense of space of
    dawn,
So many flowers beneath my every step,
I knew not where to set my careless feet!
Have you forgot the sunlight and the
    dew,
Dew in the leaves, and laughter of the
    sea?
The sea but now was laughing as it laughs
On days whereon it knows the wind of
    joy,
And all its thousand ripples approved my
    feet,
Its ripples singing on the sands of light. . . .

      [*At this moment one of the drops of
        water which drip incessantly
        from the roof falls upon the
        flame of the lamp which* ARDI-
        ANE *holds before her, as she*

44

*turns towards the mouth of the
subterranean passage, and the
light flickers and is extinguished. The NURSE gives a
cry of terror, and ARDIANE
stops, dismayed.*

ARDIANE (*in the darkness*)

O, but where are you?

SELYSETTE

Hither: take my hand.
Stay by me: water, stagnant and profound,
Lies yonder.

ARDIANE

What, and you can see it still?

SELYSETTE

Yes, we have lived so long in darkness
here.

Ardiane and Barbe Bleue

BELLANGERE

Come hither : it is lighter here by far.

SELYSETTE

Yes, let us all go thither to the light.

ARDIANE

Then is there in this deepest darkness
    light ?

SELYSETTE

Yes, there is light. Do you not see it
    there,
A wide, pale glow illumining the depth
Beyond the further arches ?

ARDIANE

                Where ?

SELYSETTE

                O blind !
O, let me kiss you. . . .

Ardiane and Barbe Bleue

ARDIANE

Yes, there is indeed
A faint light, growing wider. . . .

SELYSETTE

O no, no!
It is your eyes, your lovely astonished eyes
That widen!

ARDIANE

O, whence is it?

MELISANDE

We do not know.

ARDIANE

But we must know!
[*She goes toward the back of the scene,
and moves to and fro, feeling
along the wall with her hands.*
Here is the wall . . . and here . . .
But higher . . . here . . . it is no longer
stone!

Ardiane and Barbe Bleue

Help me to mount upon this mass of
  rock !

> [*She climbs, supported by the others.*

Here it is like an altar.   Here the roof
Is moulded in a pointed arch. . . . And
  here—
O, O, enormous bolts and iron bars !
You have sought to push them ?   Have
  you ?

SELYSETTE

                         Never !   No !
No, never touch them : for they say the
  sea
Washes the walls — great waves will
  tumble in !
It is the sea that makes it glimmer
  green !

YGRAINE

We have so often heard it : have a
  care !

Ardiane and Barbe Bleue

MELISANDE

O, I see water tremble above our heads!

ARDIANE

No, no, it is the light that seeks you out!

BELLANGERE

She is trying to force it open!
> [*The terrified women recoil, and take
> refuge behind a great column,
> whence they follow with widened
> eyes* ARDIANE'S *every movement.*

ARDIANE

My poor sisters!
Why, if you love your darkness, do you
seek
Deliverance from any quarter? Why,
If you were happy, did you use to
weep?

49

O, the bars rise! They rise! And now
    the doors
Are going to open! Wait!
       [And indeed the heavy panels of a
       sort of great interior shutter are
       seen, while yet she is speaking,
       to open, but as yet only a very
       faint, diffused, and sombre light
       illuminates the round aperture
       perceived under the vaulted
       ceiling.

      ARDIANE (*continuing her search*)
               No light as yet,
No real light! But now I pass
My   hands   across. . . . What is it?
    Glass?
Or maybe marble. . . . One would say
This were a window, sealed away,
Blackened with pitch. . . . My nails are
    broken! Nay,
Where are your distaffs? Melisande,

Ardiane and Barbe Bleue

Selysette, give me in my hand
A distaff : nay, a stone,
A single pebble of the thousands strown
Over the floor. . . .

    [SELYSETTE *runs to* ARDIANE, *holding
up to her a stone, which she takes.*

            Behold before your eyes
The key of your sunrise!

    [*She strikes a violent blow upon the
    glass. One of the square panes
    is shattered into fragments, and
    a great dazzling star seems to
    burst forth in the darkness.
    The women give a cry of
    almost delighted terror, and
    ARDIANE, now beside herself,
    and wholly submerged in a
    more and more intolerable
    radiance, breaks all the re-
    maining panes with heavy,
    hurried blows, in a kind of
    ecstatic delirium.*

Ardiane and Barbe Bleue

Yet another pane!
Now, and now again!
Till they fall, great and small, shattered,
    down to the last of all!
All the panes in ruin crack,
And O the flames are driving back
My hands, my hair!
I can see nothing now of what is
    there!
Nor do I longer dare
To raise my lids, for now it seems
They are mad with fury, the dazzling
    beams!
Stir not from where you were!
I can no longer stand upright,
But shut my eyes behold the sight
Of bright long strings of pearls, my eye-
    lids lashing!
I know not what assails me, o'er me
    dashing:
Is it the skies or else the seas,
Is it the light or else the breeze?

Ardiane and Barbe Bleue

All my tresses bright have grown a torrent
    of light,
And miracle all over me is flashing!
I see no longer, but I hear
A myriad rays of light beating on either
    ear!
But how to hide my eyes I do not know,
For no shade now my two hands throw;
My eyelids dazzle me; my arms, that
    try
To cover them, do cover, but with light!
Where are you? Hither, all of you! for I
    for I
Am helpless to descend; I cannot see
    aright;
I see not, know not, where to press
My feet amid the surf of fire that sway
    my dress!
Come hither, hither all, or I shall fall
Into your darkness!

      [*At this cry* Selysette *and* Meli-
        sande *leave the shadows where-*

Ardiane and Barbe Bleue

*in they had taken refuge, and
run to the window, their hands
pressed upon their eyes, as
though to pass through flame;
and thus, groping in the light,
they mount beside* ARDIANE *on
the mass of rock. The others
follow them, and do as they;
and thus all crowd together
in the stream of blinding radiance, which forces them to
lower their heads. Then passes
a moment of dazzled silence,
during which is heard the murmur of the sea without, the
caress of the wind among grasses,
the song of birds, and the bells
of a flock of sheep going by in a
distant pasture.*

SELYSETTE

I can hear the sea!

54

Ardiane and Barbe Bleue

MELISANDE

And I can see the sky. . . .
> [*Covering her eyes with the bend of
> her arm.*

One cannot look !

ARDIANE

My eyes are growing calmer 'neath my
hands.
Where are we ?

BELLANGERE

Trees are all that I would see.
Where are they ?

YGRAINE

O, but how the world is green !

ARDIANE

We are midway upon the cliff-side here.

55

Ardiane and Barbe Bleue

MELISANDE

Down there—the village! Do you see
    the village?

BELLANGERE

We cannot reach the village: all around
Is water, and the bridges all up-drawn.

SELYSETTE

Where are there people?

MELISANDE

        There is a peasant there —
Yonder.

SELYSETTE

He saw—is looking at us now.
See, I will make a sign to him. . . .
           [She waves her long hair.
                 He saw!
He saw my hair, he takes his bonnet off!
He makes the sign of the Cross!

Ardiane and Barbe Bleue

MELISANDE

A bell, a bell! [*Counting the strokes.*
Seven, eight, nine!

BELLANGERE

Ten . . . and eleven . . . twelve!

MELISANDE

So it is noon. . . .

YGRAINE

Who is it singing so?

MELISANDE

Why, those are birds! Do you see them?
        There they are!
There are thousands in the lofty poplar
        trees
That grow along the river.

Ardiane and Barbe Bleue

SELYSETTE

Alladine!
Where is she, O where is she, Alladine?
For I would kiss her.

MELISANDE

Alladine is here,
And I, I kiss her.

SELYSETTE

You—O Melisande,
You are so pale!

MELISANDE

You also, you are pale!
No, do not look at me!

SELYSETTE

And see, your dress
Is all in tatters: I can see you through
it. . . .

Ardiane and Barbe Bleue

MELISANDE

And yours; for your uncovered breasts appear,
Parting your tresses. . . . Do not look at me.

BELLANGERE

How long our tresses are!

YGRAINE

How pale our cheeks!

BELLANGERE

The sun shines through our hands. . . .

MELISANDE

O, Alladine!
She is sobbing!

SELYSETTE

I am kissing, kissing her. . . .

ARDIANE

Ah yes, kiss one another: do not yet
Look in each other's faces: more than all

Ardiane and Barbe Bleue

You shall not think that light will make
    you sad.
You shall by your intoxication profit
To issue from the tomb. Here steps of
    stone
Descend the cliff-side. Though I do not
    know
Whither they lead, yet they are full of
    light,
And the free winds of heaven assail them.
    Come !
Follow me all ! A thousand thousand rays
Are dancing, dancing on the crests of the
    sea !

        [*She goes out through the opening
          and disappears in the light
          without.*

SELYSETTE (*who follows, drawing the
       others after her*)

Come, yes, O come, my poor, my happy
    sisters !

Ardiane and Barbe Bleue

Let us too dance, dance, dance the dance
   of the light !
     [They all climb the great stone and
       disappear, singing in the brilli-
       ance of outer day.

THE RECEDING VOICES

Orlamonde's five daughters
   (The faery's days were o'er),
Orlamonde's five daughters
   Found at last the door.

CURTAIN

ACT THE THIRD

*The curtain rises on the same scene as in the
First Act. The scattered jewels are
still glistening in the niches, and on
the marble floor. Between the pillars
of the semi-circular colonnade are open
coffers, overflowing with costly raiment.
It is now night without, and under the
hanging candelabra, the tapers of
which are lit, ALLADINE, SELYSETTE,
MELISANDE, YGRAINE and BELLANGERE
are standing before the great mirrors,
and each is giving the touches of com-
pletion to the dressing of her hair, or
adjusting the folds of her glittering
attire, or decking herself with jewels
and flowers, while ARDIANE, passing*

Ardiane and Barbe Bleue

*from one to the other, assists and
advises them all. The great windows
are open.*

Selysette

Though from the spell-bound castle we
    as yet
Discover no escape, yet wherefore fear,
Since he is here no longer ?

                [Embracing Ardiane.

                    We are happy,
And still, because you tarry with us, free.

Melisande

Where has he gone ?

Ardiane

              I know no more than you.
Yet gone he has.   It may be he is troubled :
It may be for the first time disconcerted.
It well may be the anger of the peasants

Ardiane and Barbe Bleue

Left him uneasy ; he has felt their hate
Brim over : who shall say he has not gone
To search out guards or soldiers to chastise
The mutinous, and so return a master ?

Melisande

You will not go away ?

Ardiane

                        How should I go,
When all the castle moats are brimming
        full,
When all the drawbridges are hoisted high,
When all the doors and gates are locked
        and barred,
When all the walls are inaccessible ?
Though none are seen to guard them,
        none the less
The doors are not abandoned ; all our steps
Are closely spied ; he must have given out
Mysterious orders.   But on every side

64

Ardiane and Barbe Bleue

The peasants wait and watch upon the
 roads.
Meanwhile, my sisters, the eventful hour
Draws nigh ; we must be very beautiful.
But is it so that you prepare yourselves?
Your hair was full of miracle, Melisande !
Below, it lit the darkness of the vaults,
Steadfast it smiled upon the night of the
 tomb,
And now you have extinguished every
 flame !
Again I come to liberate the light !

> [*She removes* MELISANDE'S *veil,
> cuts with her scissors the fillets
> that constrain her tresses, and
> all her hair suddenly flows
> downwards, streaming resplen-
> dent over her shoulders.*

 YGRAINE (*turning about to look at*
    MELISANDE)
O !

Ardiane and Barbe Bleue

SELYSETTE (*also turning*)

I can hardly think it still is she !
She is so beautiful !

ARDIANE

And you, and you
Those loveliest arms, where are they, Sely
sette ?
What have you done ?

SELYSETTE

Within my silver sleeves
Here are my arms.

ARDIANE

I cannot see them, no,
Not as I saw them but a while ago,
Saw those arms I worshipped so,
The while I watched you, saw you dress,
Every strand and every tress ;
They seemed as they were raised above

Your head to reach, to appeal for love.
My loving eyes caressed your every gesture :
I turned about, and when I turn again
I see their shadow merely through their
    vesture
That shone but now so bright.   But now
    these twain
Twin rays of happiness I liberate !
             [*She detaches the sleeves.*

SELYSETTE

My poor bare arms !   O, they will shake
    with cold !

ARDIANE

No, for they are too beautiful !   And
    you,
             [*Turning to* YGRAINE.
Ygraine, where are you ?   For there shone
    but now,
Deep in this mirror, shoulders, and a
    throat,

That flooded it with happy, tender
    light :
Come, I must liberate you all ! My
    sisters,
In truth I do not wonder any more
He never loved you as he should have
    loved,
Or that he coveted a hundred, yet
Possessed no woman.

> [*Removing the mantle that* YGRAINE
> *has thrown over her shoulders.*

           O two fountain-heads
Of beauty into darkness cast away !
This above all : fear nothing ! And
    to-night
Let us be beautiful !

> [*The* NURSE, *haggard and dishevelled,*
> *enters by a side door.*

THE NURSE

           O, he is here !
He is returning !

Ardiane and Barbe Bleue

THE OTHERS

Who? Who? He? To-night?

ARDIANE

Who told you?

SELYSETTE

Were you able to go out?

ARDIANE

Have you seen any one?

THE NURSE

Yes, yes, a guard!
He has seen you, he admires you!

ARDIANE

I have seen
No creature since the hour he went away.
All gates, all doors of their own motion
    close,
Though none knows how; the palace
    seems deserted.

Ardiane and Barbe Bleue

THE NURSE

They hide, I say they hide,
And we are all espied
Forever here.
It was the youngest spoke to me;
He is returning; he must be,
He said, quite near.
The peasants are in arms. The peasants
    know!
They are rising! All the village is below,
Lurking among the hedges! Hark! A
    cry!

> [*She mounts by one of the curving
>   lateral stairways to the win-
>   dows of the gallery.*

There are torches in the copses going by!

> [*The women, terrified, give a cry of
>   horror, and run to and fro
>   through the hall, seeking a
>   point of exit. The* NURSE *en-*
>   *deavours to stop them.*

Ardiane and Barbe Bleue

The Nurse

Seek not to fly: you know the doors are
    shut.
Where would you go? Stay here, stay
    here, and wait!

Selysette (*also mounting to the windows*)

O, the great chariot! It is stopping!
       [*All mount the stairs to the windows,
         crowding together on the in-
         terior balcony, and leaning out
         into the night.*

Melisande

                    See!
Now he steps out! I see him! And he
    makes
Signs, signs of anger!

Selysette

            All around him stand
His negroes!

Ardiane and Barbe Bleue

MELISANDE

And they all have naked swords
That glitter in the moon !

SELYSETTE (*taking refuge in* ARDIANE'S *arms*)

O Ardiane !
O Ardiane, I am frightened !

THE NURSE

Do you see ?
The peasants are appearing !   There they
come !
See, there again !   And O, they have their
scythes,
Their pitch-forks !

SELYSETTE

They are going to fight !
[*Murmurs, cries, uproar, tumult,
blasphemy, and the clashing of
arms in the distance without.*

72

Ardiane and Barbe Bleue

MELISANDE

They fight!

YGRAINE

One of the negroes there has fallen!

THE NURSE

O,

The peasants, they are terrible! Their
scythes!
They are so huge! And all the village
there!

MELISANDE

O look, the negroes are deserting him!
They fly, they fly! They are hiding in
the woods!

YGRAINE

And he is flying also! Now he runs!
Now he is making for the castle court!

THE NURSE

The peasants after him!

73

Ardiane and Barbe Bleue

SELYSETTE

O, they will kill him!

THE NURSE

They are going out to help him! See
the guards!
They have opened wide the castle gates!
They run!
They run to help him!

SELYSETTE

One, two, three, four, five . . .
Now six . . . now seven. . . . There
are only seven!

THE NURSE

O look, the peasants are surrounding
them!
They are there in hundreds!

MELISANDE

O, what are they doing?

Ardiane and Barbe Bleue

THE NURSE

I see them dancing round about a man:
The rest have fallen!

SELYSETTE

     And the man is he!
I caught a sight of his blue mantle
  then:
He is lying on the grass!

THE NURSE

      Now they are still!
Now they are raising him!

MELISANDE

        O, is he hurt?

YGRAINE

He staggers!

SELYSETTE

    He is bleeding! I saw blood!
Ardiane!

Ardiane and Barbe Bleue

ARDIANE

      Come away then, look no more!
Hide your head here in my arms!

THE NURSE

        They are bringing ropes!
They are disputing! Now they tie his
    limbs!

MELISANDE

Where are they going? For they carry
    him. . . .
They are dancing, they are singing!

THE NURSE

          Hither, see!
They are coming hither : see them on the
    bridge!
The gates are open. They are halting. O,
They mean to cast him in the moat!

Ardiane and Barbe Bleue

ARDIANE AND THE OTHERS (*terrified, crying aloud, and rocking to and fro in desperation at the windows*)

No, no!
Help, help him! Do not kill him!
Help him, help!
No, no, not that! Not that! Not that!
Not that!

THE NURSE

They do not hear. . . . The others thrust them on. . . .

ARDIANE

He is saved!

THE NURSE

And now they are before the gate,
And now they seek to break into the yard!

[*Cries from the* CROWD, *who have caught sight of the women at the windows. They then sing.*

77

Ardiane and Barbe Bleue

Open! Open! Open! Open the door!
Open wide the door!
Open in God's name!
The candle gutters o'er,
The wick has no more flame!

THE WOMEN

We cannot! . . . It is barred! . . . They
break it in!
Hear it give way! They all are coming
in!
And now they struggle up the flight of
steps
Before the door below. . . . Beware!
Beware!
They are all drunken!

ARDIANE

I am going now
To unbar the door below. . . .

78

Ardiane and Barbe Bleue

THE OTHERS

O Ardiane ! [*Terrified and imploring.*
No ! They are drunken ! Bolt it, Ardiane !
They are at the door !

ARDIANE

Fear nothing : stay you there.
Do not come down, for I will go alone.

[*The five women descend the stairs
which lead down from the windows, and recoil towards the
nearer end of the hall, and
there remain, grouped rigidly
together in an attitude of terrified attention.* ARDIANE, *followed by the* NURSE, *goes to the
great central door, under the
colonnade, and throws back both
leaves of it. There is a sound
of trampling feet, of shouting,
singing, and laughter. The*

79

foremost members of the crowd appear, amid the red glare of the torches, as it were framed in the doorway, which they entirely fill, but without crossing the threshold. They are folk of brutal appearance, savage or hilarious according to disposition; their clothes are torn and disordered after their struggle. They are carrying BARBE BLEUE, *who is tightly pinioned, and pause for a moment, disconcerted at the appearance of* ARDIANE, *who is standing before them grave, unperturbed, and imperial. At the same time, further back among those peasants who are crowded together on the flight of steps, and cannot see what is passing, there are cries, sudden*

Ardiane and Barbe Bleue

> *thrusts and pushes, shouts, and laughter that lasts a moment and is then extinguished by the perplexed and respectful whisperings of those about the door. At the moment of the invasion of the doorway by the crowd, the five women silently and instinctively fall on their knees at the end of the hall remoter from the door.*

AN OLD PEASANT (*removing his bonnet and rolling it in his hands*)
Well, lady, can a man come in?

ONE OF THOSE THAT CARRY BARBE BLEUE
You see,
He'll do you no more ill!

A THIRD PEASANT
He's heavy. . . . Ouf!

Ardiane and Barbe Bleue

THE FIRST PEASANT
Where would you have us put him?

ANOTHER PEASANT
                              Over there
Down in the corner.
                    [*They lay* BARBE BLEUE *down.*
                    There now, there he lies!
Now he will never stir again!   No more!
Much evil has he done us!

ANOTHER PEASANT
                              Have you got
Somewhat to kill him with?

ARDIANE
                    Yes, never fear. . . .

THE PEASANT
Will you have some one help you?

Ardiane and Barbe Bleue

ARDIANE

No, no need. . . .
We shall do well.

A PEASANT

But look you have a care :
Beware lest he escape you !

[*Baring his chest.*
See you now,
What he has done to me !

ANOTHER PEASANT (*baring his arm*)

Now see my arm !
It came in here, and then out there it
went.

ARDIANE

You are all brave folk, but do you leave
us now.
We shall avenge ourselves, and well ; but
now

83

Ardiane and Barbe Bleue

Leave us, I pray, for night is growing
    late,
And see to all your wounds.

THE OLD PEASANT

               Now show respect,
Because we are not savages, to ladies.
We shall not make a sound. . . . It is not,
    lady,
Words, merely—but you are too beautiful.
Good-bye, good-bye.

ARDIANE (*closing the door*)

      Good-bye ; you have my thanks.
    [*She turns and sees the five
       women on their knees at the
       other end of the hall.*
You were on your knees !
        [*Approaching* BARBE BLEUE.
      And you are wounded ? Yes !
The blood is flowing here—'tis in the
    neck—

Ardiane and Barbe Bleue

'Tis nothing ; no, the wound is shallow.
    This,
Here on the arm—but hurts upon the
    arm
Are seldom very grave—but as for
    this—
The bleeding will not stop : the hand is
    pierced.
First we must dress it.

> [*While* ARDIANE *is speaking the
> five women draw nigh, one
> by one, and without speaking
> kneel or l*e*an about* BARBE
> BLEUE.

SELYSETTE

His eyes are open now.

MELISANDE

How pale he is !   He must have suffered !

Ardiane and Barbe Bleue

SELYSETTE

O!
Those peasants are so terrible!

ARDIANE

Some water!

THE NURSE

Yes, I will go and seek some. . . .

ARDIANE

Have you linen?

MELISANDE

Here is my kerchief.

SELYSETTE

He is stifling!   O,
Would you not have me hold his head up?

Ardiane and Barbe Bleue

MELISANDE

Stay,

See, I will help you.

SELYSETTE

No, for Alladine
Is helping me.

[ALLADINE *indeed is helping her to
raise* BARBE BLEUE'S *head, and
she furtively kisses his forehead,
sobbing the while.*

MELISANDE

O softly, Alladine!
What are you doing?

SELYSETTE

How his forehead burns!

Ardiane and Barbe Bleue

MELISANDE

His beard is shaven, and he is not now
So terrible. . . .

SELYSETTE

     Have you not some water? See,
His face is covered all with dust and
   blood.

YGRAINE

He breathes with effort. . . .

ARDIANE

        Yes, it is these cords,
They stifle him. The bonds are drawn
   so tight
A rock would crumble in them. . . .
    Have you not,
Some one, a knife?

Ardiane and Barbe Blue

YGRAINE

Two knives were on the table. . .
Here is the larger.

> [*She gives it to* ARDIANE.

THE NURSE (*who has returned with the
water—terrified*)
> You are going to . . .

ARDIANE

Yes.

THE NURSE

But he is not—you see . . . he looks at
us!

ARDIANE

Raise well the cord, so I may do no
hurt. . . .

> [*One by one she cuts the bonds which
> imprison* BARBE BLEUE. *When*

she comes to those that pinion
his arms behind his back the
Nurse seizes her hands to check
her.

The Nurse

Wait till he speaks . . . we do not know
at all . . .

Ardiane

Have you another knife? This blade
is broken. . . .
The cords are very hard.

Melisande (*giving her the knife*)

Here is the other.

Ardiane

Thank you !

[*She cuts the last turns of the cord*
Silence: the beating of their

Ardiane and Barbe Bleue

hearts is heard. BARBE BLEUE,
*feeling himself free, rises slowly
to a sitting posture, his arms
still benumbed, and moves his
hands to make them supple.
He then regards each of the
women about him fixedly, and in
silence. Then, leaning against
the wall, he stands upright and
remains motionless, looking at
his injured hand.*

ARDIANE (*drawing near to him*)

Good-bye.

[*She kisses him upon the brow.*
BARBE BLEUE *makes an in-
stinctive movement to detain
her. She gently frees herself,
and proceeds toward the door,
followed by the* NURSE.

Ardiane and Barbe Bleue

SELYSETTE (*running after her and stopping her*)

       Ardiane, Ardiane!
Where are you going?

     ARDIANE

      Far away from here,
Down yonder, where I am awaited still. . . .
Do you come with me, Selysette?

     SELYSETTE

        I too?
But when will you return?

     ARDIANE

      I shall not.

     MELISANDE

         O!
Ardiane!

Ardiane and Barbe Bleue

ARDIANE

Are you coming, Melisande?

[MELISANDE *looks to and fro from*
ARDIANE *to* BARBE BLEUE *and
does not reply.*

O see the open door, the far blue hills!
Ygraine, are you not coming?

[YGRAINE *does not turn her head.*

Now the moon,
The stars, illumine every road.   And you,
Bellangere, do you come?

BELLANGERE (*shortly*)

No. . . .

ARDIANE

Alladine,
Do I go forth alone?

[*At these words* ALLADINE *runs to*
ARDIANE, *throws herself into
her arms, sobbing convulsively,
and holds her in a long and
feverish embrace.*

Ardiane and Barbe Bleue

ARDIANE (*embracing her in turn, and softly disengaging herself, in tears*)

You too remain, Alladine! O be happy! And farewell. . . .

> [*She goes out hastily, followed by the* NURSE. *The five women look at one another and at* BARBE BLEUE, *who slowly raises his head.* BELLANGERE *and* YGRAINE *shrug their shoulders, and go to close the door. Silence.*

THE CURTAIN FALLS

THE END OF ARDIANE AND BARBE BLEUE